Daisy Dawson

at the Beach

DAISY DAWSON BOOKS

Daisy Dawson Is on Her Way!
Daisy Dawson and the Secret Pond
Daisy Dawson and the Big Freeze
Daisy Dawson at the Beach

Daisy Dawson
at the Beach

Steve Voake
illustrated by Jessica Meserve

CANDLEWICK PRESS

Contents

Chapter 1   Summer Vacation   1

Chapter 2   Morning Visitors   11

Chapter 3   Rabsy and Raberta   19

Chapter 4   Dancing with Pinchy   29

Chapter 5   Dolphin in Danger   51

Chapter 6   Rescuing Rabbits   65

Chapter 7   Raindrops and Rainbows   79

Chapter 1
Summer Vacation

It was the last day of school, and Daisy was saying good-bye to the class gerbils, Burble and Furball.

"Can we stay with you for the summer?" asked Furball. "We could invite the squirrels over for a sleepover and watch movies about gerbils who save the world."

"Sorry," said Daisy. "I'm going on vacation tomorrow, so Abigail's going to look after you."

"Does she have any movies about gerbils saving the world?" asked Burble.

"I don't think so," said Daisy, "but she does have popcorn."

"Ooh," said Furball. "I like her already."

"It doesn't take much to make him happy," said Burble. She waved at Daisy through the bars. "Have a great summer, Daisy D!"

"You, too!" said Daisy.

As she walked home, she noticed Trixie the cat sneaking through the long grass toward Flapperton, a sparrow. Daisy had made friends with Flapperton only that morning when she had given him some of her pancake.

"Hey, Trixie!" she called as loudly as she could. "What are you up to?"

As Flapperton squawked
and flew up into the
trees, Trixie stared
at Daisy with cool
green eyes.

"Thanks a bunch, Daisy,"
she said. "How would you like it if
I scared your dinner away?"

Daisy smiled sweetly. "You're welcome
to try," she said, "but I don't think peanut-
butter sandwiches scare easily."

"You didn't upset her, did you?" chuckled
Boom the dog as Trixie slunk away again
into the long grass. "I really hate it when
cats get upset." He put his paws on the fence
and rested his chin on the warm wood.
"How was school?"

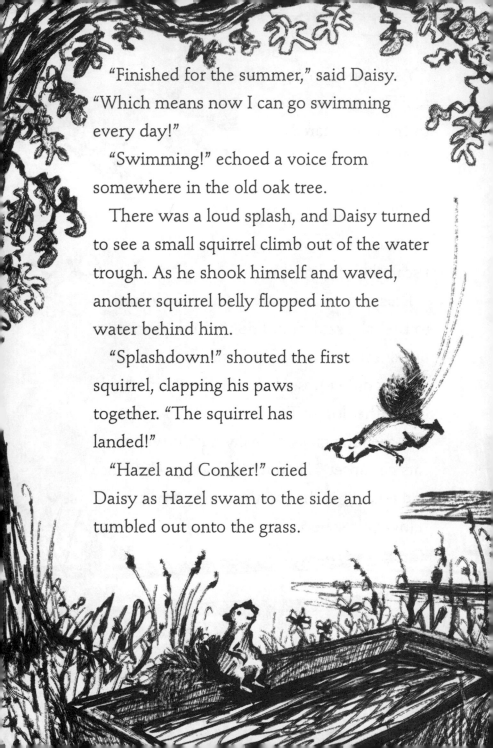

"Finished for the summer," said Daisy. "Which means now I can go swimming every day!"

"Swimming!" echoed a voice from somewhere in the old oak tree.

There was a loud splash, and Daisy turned to see a small squirrel climb out of the water trough. As he shook himself and waved, another squirrel belly flopped into the water behind him.

"Splashdown!" shouted the first squirrel, clapping his paws together. "The squirrel has landed!"

"Hazel and Conker!" cried Daisy as Hazel swam to the side and tumbled out onto the grass.

"Hello, Daisy," said Conker, squeezing the water out of his tail. "Want to go for a swim?"

"Thanks for the offer," said Daisy, "but I think I'll wait until I get to the seashore."

"Seashore?" said Hazel, drying herself with a leaf. "What's a seashore?"

"You know," said Conker. "That thing in the park that goes up and down."

"The sun?" said Hazel.

"I think he means a see*saw,*" said Daisy.

"That's it," said Conker. "I've always wanted to go on one."

"I'm talking about the sea*shore,*" explained Daisy patiently. Conker looked confused.

"It's also called a beach," she added helpfully. "It's a place with water and boats and ice cream."

"Is it very scary at the beach?" asked Hazel.

"No, it's great," said Daisy. "Why?"

"Because you said it makes you scream."

"Huh?" said Conker.

"You said 'It's a place with lots of boats and water and I scream.'"

"No, not 'I scream,'" said Daisy. "Ice cream."

"I know. That's what I said."

Daisy shook her head. "No, *ice cream*. You know when the water trough freezes over in winter?"

"Uh-huh."

"Well, it's a little like that."

"Can you skate on it?"

"Not really. You sort of . . . eat it."

"Wow," said Conker. "This beach place is *nuts*." He stared at Daisy for a moment and then asked, "Where's that funny thing you put all your stuff in?"

Daisy glanced over her shoulder and realized that Conker was talking about her backpack.

"I put it down over there," she said, pointing, "but I won't need it now since school is out for the summer."

At that moment, Meadowsweet the mare trotted out from beneath the oak tree and leaned over the fence to nuzzle Daisy's hair.

"Hello, Meadowsweet," said Daisy. "I was just telling everyone that I'm going to the beach tomorrow."

"How lovely," said Meadowsweet. "I knew a donkey who went there once. He wore a straw hat to keep the sun off his head, and he used to let the children ride around on his back."

"That sounds like fun," said Conker, looking up at Meadowsweet.

"Don't get any ideas, young squirrel," said Meadowsweet. "It's too hot for that kind of thing."

"Is the water there as big as the river?" asked Boom.

"It's called the ocean, and it's bigger than the river," said Daisy. "Sometimes you can see the whole sky in it."

"The whole sky," whispered Hazel. "Imagine that."

Daisy saw that Boom was looking worried and remembered Meadowsweet telling

her that he had once fallen into deep water
as a puppy.

"Don't worry, Boom," she said. "I'm a
really good swimmer."

As she knelt down and stroked his ears, he
whispered, "The ocean's a big place, Daisy.
Promise me if you ever get lost in it, you'll
swim toward the sun."

"The sun?" Daisy frowned. "Why?"

"Because the sun's above the field," said
Boom. "And if you swim toward it, you'll
find your way home."

Chapter 2
Morning Visitors

Daisy was dreaming of blue skies and sandy beaches when she woke to the sound of a bird coughing. When she pulled back the curtains, she saw Flapperton on the windowsill, slapping a small sparrow on the back with his wing.

"Ooh, that's it," said the smaller sparrow. "A little to the left, maybe."

"Is everything all right?" asked Daisy, opening the window. Although she had become used to talking animals, this was the first time she had ever been woken up by a coughing sparrow.

"Oh, hi, Daisy," said Flapperton. "Thanks for saving me from that cat yesterday, by the way."

"That's OK," said Daisy. "What's the matter with your friend?"

"It's a toast crust," Flapperton explained. "Harry here tried to eat the whole thing, but it got stuck in his throat."

Harry coughed a bit more. Then he put his wing over his beak, because his mother had taught him that this was the polite thing to do.

"Hang on," said Daisy. "Be back in a second."

She raced downstairs to the kitchen, where her mom and dad were setting the table for breakfast.

"You're up bright and early," said Dad.

"Going to help pack the van?"

It was then Daisy remembered that they were going on their camping trip today. For a moment she was so excited, she forgot why she had come downstairs.

"Should I get the surfboard?" she asked. "And the snorkels and masks?"

"That would be good," said Dad, looking at her pajamas. "But maybe the first thing you should get is . . . dressed."

"Have some breakfast first," said Mom. "I'll make some more toast."

The thought of toast reminded Daisy what she had come down for. She opened the fridge, took out a bottle of orange soda, and headed back upstairs.

"Soda for breakfast?" said Mom. "I'm not sure that's a good idea."

"Absolutely not," said Dad.

He opened the fridge and peered inside.

"I don't suppose there's any left?"

"Hold still, Harry," said Daisy, picking up the little sparrow in her left hand.

Harry coughed and looked up at her. "Will it hurt?" he asked.

"Not at all," replied Daisy, "although it might make your beak tingle for a while. Ready?"

Harry nodded and shut his eyes as Daisy tipped the first few drops into his beak.

At first, nothing happened. Then Harry gave a little squawk and began to dance around on Daisy's hand, flapping his wings and chirruping loudly.

"Is he all right?" asked Flapperton. "He seems a bit . . . bonkers."

"That's just the fizz," said Daisy. "He'll be fine."

"Whoo-hoo!" exclaimed Harry, staggering sideways as Daisy set him down on the windowsill. "That got those crumbs!"

"All clear?" asked Flapperton.

"You betcha," said Harry. "Throat clear, eyes clear, head clear. And my beak's all bibbly-bubbly. Thanks, Daisy!"

"No problem," said Daisy. "Now promise me you'll go easy on those crusts."

"Promise," said Harry, and flew off to do a figure eight around the chimney pots.

"You could come and watch us fly around the park if you like," said Flapperton. "I'm going to show Harry how to do loop-the-loops."

"Normally I'd love

to," said Daisy, "but I'm going to the beach today."

"The beach? That's near the ocean, isn't it?" Daisy nodded. Flapperton was quiet for a moment. Then he said, "I met some swifts once who told me stories about the ocean. They used to fly thousands of miles to distant lands. And one day, when they were skimming across the ocean, they flew through a rainbow and the whole sky was alive with colors. Can you imagine anything more wonderful?"

"It sounds nice," agreed Daisy.

"The thing is," said Flapperton, "although I practice every day, I know I'll never be able to fly as far or as high as they do. But I still dream about it, Daisy. I still dream about flying through rainbows."

As he looked at her, Daisy saw the bright sky reflected in his eyes.

"Will you tell me about it?" he asked.

"When you come back, will you tell me about all the things you've seen?"

Daisy smiled. "Of course I will," she said.

She watched him fly away across the rooftops, then closed the window and clapped her hands together.

"Time to start packing!" she said.

Chapter 3
Daisy and Roberta

After they parked at the site, Mom and Dad
started to unpack the van.

"I'll be finished soon," Mom said to Daisy.
"Then we can go down to the beach for a
swim."

"Is there anything I can do to help?" asked
Daisy.

"You could fetch some water," said Dad.
"Then I'll put on the kettle and make us a
nice cup of tea."

* * *

The campsite was on a cliff top overlooking the ocean. It was a hot, blue day, and as Daisy watched the sun sparkling on the water, she imagined running across the sand toward the waves. She guessed that most people were already on the beach, enjoying the warm sunshine.

She had just turned on the tap to fill the bucket when she heard a little voice say, "Look. It's a magical cloud lady."

"Are you sure?" asked another voice.

"Yes. She fills a cloud with rain, puts it up in the sky, and then it comes down *blib-a-loober-lub*. Like that."

Daisy turned off the faucet and looked around.

"Why did she stop?" asked the second voice.

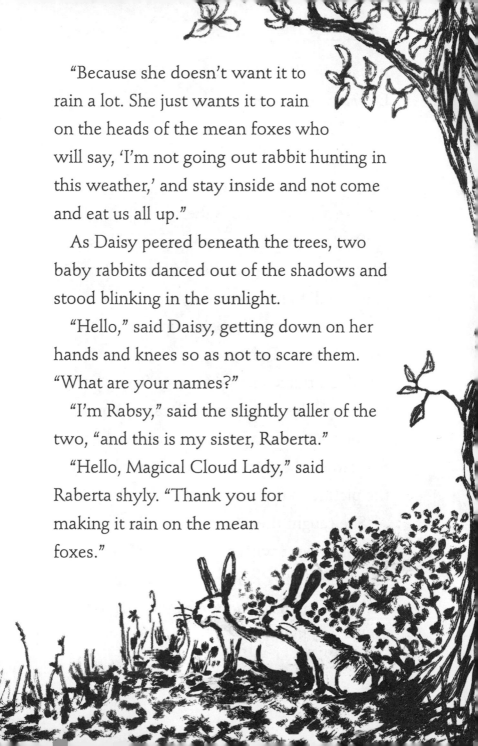

"Because she doesn't want it to
rain a lot. She just wants it to rain
on the heads of the mean foxes who
will say, 'I'm not going out rabbit hunting in
this weather,' and stay inside and not come
and eat us all up."

As Daisy peered beneath the trees, two
baby rabbits danced out of the shadows and
stood blinking in the sunlight.

"Hello," said Daisy, getting down on her
hands and knees so as not to scare them.
"What are your names?"

"I'm Rabsy," said the slightly taller of the
two, "and this is my sister, Raberta."

"Hello, Magical Cloud Lady," said
Raberta shyly. "Thank you for
making it rain on the mean
foxes."

Daisy smiled. "My name is Daisy Dawson, and I don't make it rain on the foxes," she said. She held up the bucket to show them. "This is to put water in so people can drink it later."

"Like a cloud," said Raberta.

"Well . . . yes, I guess so," agreed Daisy. "But clouds live up in the sky, and this one's going back to my campsite."

"Won't it mind not being up with all the others?" asked Rabsy.

"I don't think so," said Daisy. Then, an idea struck her. She took her camera from her pocket and snapped a picture of the sky. She turned the camera around and showed the picture to the rabbits.

"She caught them!" squeaked Raberta, hopping about with excitement. "She caught the clouds in her magical cloud catcher!"

"Shake them out so we can have a better look," said Rabsy.

"They're not really in there," Daisy
explained. "They're just pictures so you can
see them again when you get home."

"Like Rabsy, you mean?" asked Raberta.
"I always see him again when I get home.
Usually holding a carrot."

Rabsy nodded. "I like carrots," he said.

At that moment, Daisy heard her mother
calling.

"I think I'd better be getting back," she
said. "We're going surfing."

"Surfing?" asked Raberta. "What's that?"

"Oh it's a lot of fun," said Daisy. "You lie on a surfboard, and the waves take you all the way to the beach."

"What's a beach?" asked Raberta.

"That brown crumbly thing at the bottom of the cliff," said Rabsy.

"Oh," said Raberta. "And what are waves?"

"The blue uppy-downy things."

"And what's a surfboard?"

"A foam floaty thing," said Daisy.

"Oh, right." Raberta thought for a moment. "So you lie on the foam floaty thing and look at the white cloudy things until a blue uppy-downy thing takes you to the brown crumbly thing?"

"Sounds about right," said Daisy.

"Wow!" said Raberta. "Can Rabsy and I try?"

"I don't know," said Daisy. "It's not the kind of thing rabbits usually do."

"That's why we should do it," said Raberta. "I want to be the first rabbit to ride on a foam floaty thing!"

"Me, too!" said Rabsy. "I want to be first, too! Oh, can we? Please, Daisy, puh-*lease*?"

Daisy was about to say she really didn't think it would be a good idea, when she remembered how sad Flapperton the sparrow had been about the things he couldn't do. She didn't have the heart to make the rabbits sad, too.

"I tell you what," she said. "If you come down to the beach tomorrow, I'll see what I can do."

"Oh, thank you," said Raberta, hugging Daisy's leg and planting rabbity kisses all over it. *"Mwah, mwah, mwah!"*

Daisy smiled. "See you tomorrow," she said. "By the blue uppy-downy things."

* * *

"Look," said Dad as they were enjoying their tea. "Aren't those rabbits over there?"

Daisy turned to see Rabsy and Raberta standing by the bushes, gazing up at the sky.

"I could have sworn I just saw one of them point up at the clouds," he said.

"That's probably because they think I put them up there," said Daisy. "They've got amazing imaginations, those rabbits."

Dad smiled.

"They're not the only ones," he said.

Chapter 4
Dancing with Pinchy

"Did you know," said Dad, staring out at the waves, "that more than half of our bodies are made up of water?"

"Mine isn't," said Daisy, taking another bite of her sandwich. "At the moment, mine's mostly made up of peanut butter." She stood up and looked around to see if there was any sign of the rabbits. She hadn't seen them for a couple of days and wondered if they had changed their minds about learning to surf. "Can I go swimming now?"

"You'd better finish your sandwich first," said Mom. "Why don't you go and look in the tide pools? You never know what you might find."

As Daisy wandered across the sand, two seagulls landed nearby and stared at her.

"I-think-she's-got-some-food!" squawked the first one. "I-think-she's-got-some-food-I-bet-she's-got-some-food-I saw-her-with-some-food-where-did-she-put-her-food?"

"I-think-I-see-her-food!" squawked the second one. "I-think-I-see-her-food-I-do-I-see-her-food-I-want-to-have-her-food-and-you-can't-have-her-food!"

"You can both have some," said Daisy, tearing the crusts off the sandwich. "But first you have to calm down or you might choke, and I don't have any soda left."

"*Eek!*" said the first seagull.

"*Ulp!*" said the second one, shutting his beak with a loud clack.

"That's better," said Daisy, throwing them half a crust each.

"You're a funny-looking seagull," said the first one when he had finished off his bread. "Did your feathers fall off or something?"

"I'm not a seagull," said Daisy. "I just know how to talk to animals, that's all."

"You talk funny," said the first one. "You should use the back of your throat more. *Ark! Ark!* Like that."

"*Ark! Ark!*" said Daisy.

"Not bad. But you need to work on it." The seagull waddled closer. "I don't suppose you can talk to fish, can you?"

"I don't know," replied Daisy. "I've never tried."

"Well, you *should* try."

"She should try, shouldn't she?" said the other seagull.

"When you get down to the water, ask them all to swim up to the surface."

"Swim up to the surface," echoed the other seagull.

"So you can eat them, you mean?" said Daisy.

"*Ark! Ark!*" shouted the seagulls together. "Eat-the-fish! Eat-the-fish!"

"I don't think I will, thank you," said Daisy. "But it was nice to meet you!"

"I said that to a fish once," said the first seagull. "Nice to eat you! *Ark! Ark!*"

"*Ark! Ark!*" The other seagull laughed. "Nice-to-eat-you! Nice-to-eat-you!"

They both flew up into the air squawking, "Eat-the-fish! Eat-the-fish! Eat-the-fish! Eat-the-fish!"

"Honestly!" said Daisy, folding her arms. She thought about Flapperton and was glad that at least *some* birds had been brought up to have good manners.

Daisy sat on a rock next to a long, deep pool and dangled her feet in the water. She loved the way the tide went out and left its treasures hidden among the rocks: glassy shrimps tiptoeing across silver sand, bright

33

fish darting beneath the weeds, and the tiny tentacles of sea anemones waving like mermaids' hair in the watery breeze.

"Ow!" she said suddenly. "Owchy, ow, ow, ow!"

Pulling her foot from the water, she saw a small crab hanging from her toe by one of its claws. Carefully, she lowered her foot onto the rock, and the crab scuttled sideways.

"HA-HA!" it said, waving its claws at her. "PINCHY, PINCHY, PINCHY!"

"That's not very nice," said Daisy, rubbing her toe.

"What?" said the crab.

"I said it's not very nice, going around pinching people like that."

"Pinchy, pinchy, pinchy,"

said the crab again, sidling up to Daisy's toe. "Pinchy, pinchy, pinchy!"

"Now, *stop* it," said Daisy firmly, pulling her toe away. "How would you like it if I started pinching you?"

The crab stared at her. "You don't have claws," he said.

"So?" replied Daisy. She began tapping her fingers and thumbs together, then moved them toward the crab. "Pinchy, pinchy, pinchy. Pinchy, pinchy, pinchy!"

"*¡Ay, caramba!*" cried the crab, putting his claws over his head. "Stop, stop!"

"You see?" said Daisy, putting her hands down. "It's not very nice, is it?"

"OK," said the crab. "I get it."

He looked at the tide pool for a moment as if he was about to jump back in. Then he seemed to change his mind.

"Wanna learn to walk sideways like me?" he said. "It's fun. It's sideways fun!"

"I already know how to walk sideways," said Daisy.

"No, you do not," said the crab. "Not like a crab."

"I do too," said Daisy. She walked sideways along the edge of the rock, did a little twirl, and then walked back again.

"Hmmm," said the crab. "That was pretty good." He scuttled closer and stared at her. "Are you *actually* a crab?"

"No."

"But all that pinching and walking sideways. And, also, you speak the lingo."

"Well, that's another story," said Daisy. "Talking to animals is just something I do."

"And this is what *I* do," said the crab, holding out his claws. "Pinchy, pinchy, pinchy. Even my name is Pinchy!"

He stopped and tapped his claw softly against the top of his shell. "I have an idea," he said. Daisy carefully moved her foot away. "How about I stop the pinching and teach you how to dance instead?"

Daisy smiled. "Pinchy," she said. "I think that's a *wonderful* idea."

"OK, then," said Pinchy. "Watch carefully. First you put your claw in the air like you just don't care."

"You mean like this?" asked Daisy, waving a hand above her head.

"Exactly like that," said Pinchy. "And now you gotta feel the rhythm, Daisy. You gotta listen to the wind and the waves and the earth and the sky, and then you move your feet like this, and your claws like this, and then you start to dance!"

He clacked his claws together, making a *ha-cha-cha* sound. "Come on! Get with the rhythm!"

Daisy raised her arms above her head and began snapping her fingers, shuffling her feet, and twirling around.

Ha, cha, ha-cha-cha! Ha, cha, ha-cha-cha!

"Look, Pinchy!" she cried. "I'm doing it!"

"And I'm loving it," said Pinchy, lifting his legs up and down in time to the rhythm. "You're making me crazy!"

"Come on, Pinchy," called Daisy, still dancing. "Let's do the dance together!"

Pinchy began copying Daisy's movements. *Ha, cha, ha-cha-cha! Ha, cha, ha-cha-cha!*

"That's it, Pinchy!" Daisy giggled. "You've got it. You've got it!"

As they danced across the rocks, more crabs crawled out of the water to join in. *Ha, cha, ha-cha-cha! Ha, cha, ha-cha-cha!*

One started a clackety rhythm in the background, one scraped his claws rhythmically across the barnacles, and another began thumping the seaweed. The sound

was so catchy that after a while even the limpets started joining in, lifting their shells up and down in time to the beat.

Slurpy-slurp, slurpy-slurp.
Slurpy-slurpy-slurpy-slurp.

Ha, cha, ha-cha-cha! Ha, cha, ha-cha-cha!

"Hey, Daisy!" called a voice behind her. "Whatcha doin'?"

Still dancing and *ha-cha-cha*-ing, Daisy turned to see Rabsy and Raberta skipping about on the sand.

"Come and join us!" she called, holding out her foot so that one of the crabs could play a solo on her toenails. Rabsy and Raberta hopped up onto the rock, and as the crabs moved back to give them space, Raberta began to rap:

> *"We're so happy, by the sea,*
> > *Hearing all the crabs go*
> > clacker-dee-dee,
> > > *I'm Raberta, he's Rabsy,*
> > > *and we're hangin' with*
> > > *our good friend Daisy D."*

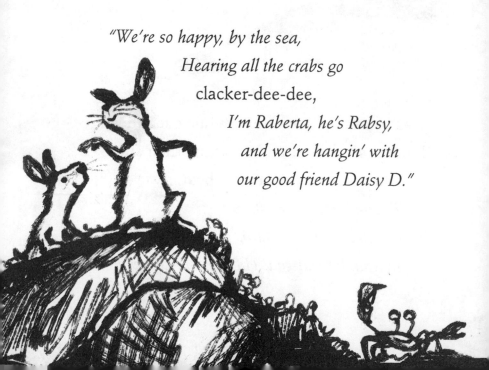

Suddenly the music stopped and all the crabs plopped back into the water just as the two seagulls swooped down onto the rock, shouting:

"Eat-the-crabs! Eat-the-crabs! Eat-the-crabs! Eat-the-crabs!"

They stopped and stared at Daisy.

"Ark! Ark! *We lost our food!*
Ark! Ark! *Well, that's no good!*
Ark! *Lunch! We came too late!* Ark! Ark!
Well, that's just great."

Then they flew away again.

"Sorry about that," said Daisy. "I don't think anyone's ever taught them to be polite."

"I don't think anyone's ever taught them how to rap, either," said Raberta. "That was awful."

"I liked the *Ark! Ark!* part," said Rabsy, skipping from foot to foot. Then he saw the way Raberta was looking at him and added, "But yours was *much* better."

Daisy looked around to see if any people had noticed the dancing crabs, but everyone seemed too busy swimming or sunbathing to pay any attention.

"*Splosh!*" said Rabsy as a wave swept into the rock pool. "The blue uppy-downy thing has come to say hello!"

"The tide's coming in," said Daisy. "Stay here while I see if I'm allowed to go surfing."

* * *

"How is the peanut-butter sandwich?" asked Dad, who was lying down reading a newspaper.

"I think it's disappeared," said Daisy, picking up her surfboard.

"Really," said Dad. "I think there

must be magic in the air."

Daisy smiled. "I think there is," she said.

"Well just be careful," said Mom. "Do you want one of us to come with you?"

"No, I'll be fine," said Daisy, who knew that trying to explain about surfing rabbits would make life complicated. "I've got my lifesaver badge, remember?"

It was true. Daisy was one of the best swimmers in her class and had placed first in the swimming competition for three years running. But even so, her parents always wanted to make sure that she was safe.

"All right," said her mom. "But stay where we can see you, and don't go out of your depth!"

When Daisy reached the water, the incoming tide had already flooded the pools, and Rabsy and Raberta were standing by the waterline playing catch with a pebble.

"You brought the foam floaty thing!" said Raberta.

"I did," said Daisy. "So who wants a ride on the blue uppy-downy things?"

"Me!" shouted both rabbits together, jumping up and down on the sand.

"OK," said Daisy, "but first you need to calm down a bit."

"Sorry," said Raberta. She stopped jumping up and down and then held on to Rabsy's ears until he stopped, too.

"Now," said Daisy, "first of all we need to go through some safety procedures."

"Do not talk to foxes," said Raberta sternly. "NEVER talk to foxes."

"OK, good," said Daisy, "although I was thinking more about surfing actually."

She did a quick check to make sure no one was watching, then waved the two rabbits toward the front of the surfboard.

"Now, go like this," she said, holding her arms out.

As Rabsy and Raberta raised their front paws, Rabsy started swaying from side to side, pretending to lose his balance.

"Uh-oh," he said. "Going . . . left! Going . . . right!"

"Rabsy, pay attention," said Daisy. "When we're riding the waves, that's when you can try to stand up. But you have to put your paws out to help you balance. And remember, any time you think you're about to fall off, just lie down and hang on to me."

"Where will you be?" asked Raberta.

"Right behind you," said Daisy. "Now let's practice. When I say 'surf,' you stand up and put your paws out, and when I say 'drop,' you lie down and pretend to be holding my arms. Are you ready?"

"Ready," said Rabsy.

"Ready," said Raberta.

"OK, and . . . surf!"

Rabsy and Raberta jumped to the front of the board and held their paws out just as they had been shown.

"And . . . drop!"

Rabsy and Raberta dropped to the board with a little *"Ooof!"* sound.

"Now pretend to be holding my arms," Daisy reminded them.

"That's it, that's it, and . . . surf! And . . .
drop! And . . . surf! And . . . drop!"

Rabsy rolled off the board and lay on his
back in the sand. "I'm tired now," he said.
"Can't we play hide-and-squeak instead?"

Daisy chewed her lip and looked out
to the water. Although she was a strong
swimmer, she could see that the waves were
rough, and she didn't want to put the little
rabbits in any danger.

"Maybe we should leave it until tomorrow," she said.

"Phew," said Rabsy, lying on his back and staring up at the sky.

"Surf's up tomorrow though, li'l brother," said Raberta, grabbing his ears and pulling him to his feet. "What d'you think, Daisy? D'you think we'll be ready to ride the blue uppy-downy things?"

Daisy smiled. "There's only one way to find out," she said.

Chapter 5
Dolphin in Danger

The next morning, Daisy met Rabsy and Raberta by the tide pools.

"I'm feeding the fish," said Rabsy, dropping bits of carrot into the water.

"I don't think fish like carrots," said Daisy.

"This one does," said Rabsy. "It's waving at me."

Daisy smiled. "That's not a fish," she explained. "It's a sea anemone. It's waving its arms around because it's trying to catch some food."

"Good thing I was here, then," said Rabsy. "Can we go surfing now?"

Daisy looked at the sea and saw that the water was much calmer than the day before. "All right," she said. "But remember the safety procedures."

"We will!" chorused the rabbits. "Surf and drop! Surf and drop!"

As Daisy pushed the surfboard through the shallow water, Rabsy and Raberta sat at the front and watched the waves gently rising and falling.

"Here comes another one!" called Rabsy, clapping his paws together as Raberta squealed with excitement. "And another! And another!"

Raberta began skipping around the surfboard, coming up with a little rap.

"We can dance and we can hop
We can surf and we can drop
But if you want to surf like me
You must be safe beside the sea.

So don't go where it's rough or deep
These are rules you have to keep."

"Excellent, Raberta," said Daisy, "but you're a little close to the edge."

"Oops, sorry," said Raberta, skipping back toward the middle of the board. "Got carried away there."

When Daisy was up to her waist in water, she turned to face the beach. Rabsy and Raberta stood at the end of the surfboard, lifting their paws just the way Daisy had shown them.

"Is this right?" squeaked Raberta. "Are we doing it right, Daisy?"

53

"That's perfect," said Daisy. "OK, ready? Here we go!"

As the ocean swelled behind her, Daisy lay on the surfboard until her arms were on either side of the two little rabbits, and then she launched herself forward. For a moment they hung on the crest of the wave, perfectly balanced between sea and sky. Then the wave broke, and they shot forward, bouncing and skimming across the water as it frothed and foamed beneath them.

"Wooooh!" cried Rabsy. *"Wheeeee!"*

"Drop, Rabsy, drop!" shouted Raberta, throwing herself forward and clinging on to Daisy's arm. But Rabsy was having so much fun that he forgot to hang on, and when the board crashed down again, he was flung off into the waves.

"Rabsy fell off!" wailed Raberta as the wave took them up the beach. "We have to go back and rescue him!"

"You stay here," said Daisy firmly. Racing back into the water, she searched frantically for the little rabbit, but all she could see was the white waves and the sunlight sparkling on the sea.

Daisy held her breath and put her face in the water, then opened her eyes, desperately searching for him. But the waves had stirred up the sand, and the salt water stung her eyes, making it impossible to see. She was

about to lift her head out of the water when she thought she heard a faint voice calling, "Help me! Help me, please!"

But when she listened again, all she could hear was the sound of the sea.

"Rabsy!" she called as she raised her head. "Rabsy, where are you?"

"Right here," said a little voice behind her. "Can you give me a lift, please?"

Daisy turned to see a bedraggled Rabsy paddling through the waves with wet fur plastered over his eyes.

"Rabsy!" she cried, scooping him up in her arms. "I thought I'd lost you!"

"I thought I'd lost me, too," said Rabsy. "But it turns out I was here all the time."

"I heard you calling for help," said Daisy as she waded through the shallow water toward the beach.

"I didn't call for help," said Rabsy. "I knew you'd come and find me." He shivered and then clapped his paws together. "That was fun! Can we do it again?"

"I think you should warm up first," said Daisy, putting him down on the sand next to Raberta. Raberta squeaked, flung her arms around him, and hugged him tightly.

As the two rabbits scampered toward the dunes to dry off in the sun, Daisy walked back up the beach, wondering where the cries for help had come from.

"You looked as if you were enjoying surfing," said Mom. "Although I could have sworn I saw something on the front of your surfboard."

"That was the rabbits," said Daisy. "They wanted to go surfing, but one of them fell off and I had to rescue him."

Mom smiled. "You and your imagination," she said.

Daisy grabbed her snorkel and mask and headed back to where she had heard the call for help. When she reached the spot, she lay on her tummy and peered down into the water. It was clearer now, and with the mask on she could see shoals of silver fish darting above the seabed. As she listened, she heard the voice again, echoing up from the depths of the ocean. "Help me," it called. "Help me, please!"

As Daisy watched patterns of sunlight dancing on the sand beneath her, she noticed that the seabed fell away into deeper, darker water. And there, lying in the shadows, was a young dolphin. It had gotten caught in an

old fishing net, and the more it struggled,
the more it became entangled.

Daisy felt completely helpless. She knew
that it was unsafe for her to swim out of her
depth. But she also knew that she couldn't
just leave the poor dolphin there.

She was about to swim back and ask her
parents for help when she heard a familiar
sound.

Ha, cha, ha-cha-cha! Ha, cha, ha-cha-cha!
Scrrrrritch! Scrrrrratch! Scrrrrritch! Scrrrrratch!
Ha, cha, ha-cha-cha! Ha, cha, ha-cha-cha!

Turning around, Daisy swam as fast as she
could toward the sound of clacking
claws. In the shallow water,
she saw a

huge assortment of crabs gathered in a circle beneath the waves. There were crabs of all shapes and sizes, from the tiniest hermit crab to a red spider crab with a huge front claw and a barnacle-encrusted shell. All of them were dancing and singing and clacking their claws in time with the music. And there, conducting the others from the middle of the circle, was someone who looked very familiar.

"Pinchy!" she cried. "Pinchy, it's me, Daisy!" Although because she had a snorkel in her mouth, it actually sounded more like, "Himp-shee! Mit's me, Nayzee!"

But it didn't matter, because as all the other crabs stopped dancing and turned to see what the ruckus was, Pinchy held up his claw and waved to her.

It was impossible to explain the situation with her snorkel in her mouth, so Daisy swam down to the seabed and held out her hand. Seeming to understand, Pinchy scuttled sideways until he was sitting on her palm, and Daisy swam to the surface again and took the snorkel out of her mouth.

"Pinchy, you've got to help me," she said.

"But why?" asked Pinchy. "You're a good dancer already."

"I'm not talking about dancing," said Daisy. "I'm talking about rescuing a dolphin."

"Ha, ha! Very funny!" said Pinchy. "Wait, I don't get it."

"I'm being serious," said Daisy. "There's a dolphin caught in a net at the bottom of the ocean, and he needs our help."

"*¡Ay, caramba!*" said Pinchy. "But Pinchy has never rescued a dolphin before."

"I'd never danced the cha-cha before, either," said Daisy. "But thanks to you, I'm pretty good at it."

"True." Pinchy clacked his claws and did a little two-step shuffle on her hand. "OK. Let me go and talk to the others."

"Please don't be long," said Daisy. "I don't think we've got much time."

Pinchy scuttled off her hand and plopped back into the water. As Daisy watched him sink to the bottom again, she felt a chill run through her and, looking up, she saw that the sun had gone behind a cloud. The sea had turned from blue to gray, and the world suddenly seemed much darker. When Daisy looked back into the water again, all she could see was swirling sand.

Daisy decided she had better swim back and tell her parents about the dolphin. They would know what to do, wouldn't they? They always knew what to do. But as she

turned toward the beach, something in the distance caught her eye.

Just around the corner in a small rocky cove, two gray dots were huddled together beneath the cliffs. They were surrounded by water, and as Daisy watched, she realized to her horror that the two dots were Rabsy and Raberta. Somehow they had managed to get stranded, and the tide was coming in.

In a few minutes, the beach where they stood would be completely underwater.

Chapter 6
Rescuing Rabbits

Without stopping to think, Daisy put her mask back on and swam as hard as she could toward the cliffs.

"Daisy! Daisy!" shouted the little rabbits when they saw her. "We're over here!"

"So I see," said Daisy, stumbling out of the water. "But what on earth are you doing here?"

"It was Rabsy's idea," said Raberta. "I said we should wait until you came back, but Rabsy said it would be all right because he was the best rabbity wave rider in the whole wide world."

"I am, too," said Rabsy.

"Uh, I don't think so," said Raberta. "The best rabbity wave riders don't crash into rocks, Rabsy."

"I don't understand," said Daisy. "You don't have a surfboard."

"I did," said Rabsy, pointing to a piece of wood that was lying next to the rocks, "but it sort of snapped."

"You went surfing on *that*?"

"I wouldn't call it surfing," said Raberta. "More like sinking."

Daisy looked at the rising water and remembered that the two little rabbits couldn't swim well. It was up to her to save them.

"Climb onto my shoulders," she instructed. "I'm going to wade past the rocks and then swim around to the beach.

Whatever you do, don't let go, OK?"

"OK," said Rabsy and Raberta. Daisy knelt down, and they scampered up onto her shoulders.

"All set?" Daisy asked as their little paws clutched at her hair.

"All set," said Rabsy and Raberta.

"OK," said Daisy. "Then, let's go!"

As the water came up to her waist, Daisy took a deep breath, pulled down her mask and launched herself forward into the ocean. The rabbits clung to her neck and Daisy could feel them shivering.

"Are we nearly there?" whispered Rabsy. "I need to go and check on my carrots."

"Soon," said Daisy, trying to reassure him.

But although she was a strong swimmer, she began to worry that the little rabbits wouldn't have the strength to hold on much longer. The sun was still behind the clouds, and the beach was far away. As Daisy looked around, all she could see was dark water around her and gray sky above her.

Then, ahead of her, a shaft of sunlight broke through the clouds.

Daisy thought of home then, of her best friend, Boom, and the sun-bright meadow behind her house. And as the water sparkled and shone like a thousand diamonds, Daisy remembered what Boom had said to her before she left.

If you swim toward the sun, you'll find your way home.

For some reason she couldn't explain, Daisy began to feel braver and stronger. Then, as she swam closer to the sunlit water, Rabsy shouted, "Look! Down there!" Daisy noticed that something was moving beneath them. It gradually rose up from the depths of the ocean, faster and faster, and then suddenly Daisy felt herself being lifted out of the water. As she looked down, she

realized to her surprise that she was on the
back of a dolphin.

"Oh!" she cried happily. "Where did *you*
come from?"

The dolphin flicked its tail, crested a wave,
and swam smoothly into calmer waters.

"I wanted to meet you," said the dolphin,
and when it spoke, Daisy thought it was
like listening to the most beautiful music she
had ever heard. "I wanted to thank you for
telling the crabs I was in trouble. They came
in their hundreds to free me from the net,
and so now you must tell me what I can do
for you in return."

"Could you take us back to the beach?" asked Daisy. "If it's not too much trouble."

"For you, nothing is too much trouble," replied the dolphin. "But perhaps you would like to come for a ride first?"

"Yes, please," whispered Daisy.

As the dolphin leaped through the waves, Daisy held on tightly and watched the water rushing past. But although they were moving at a great speed, the dolphin swam so smoothly that Daisy felt as if she were sliding through fields of blue silk. High above her, the clouds gave way to clear skies, and Daisy felt the warm sun on her back once again. Then, as they splashed across the tops of the waves, Rabsy and Raberta squealed with delight, and Daisy

turned to see tiny rainbows dancing in the spray all around them.

"They've got green grass in them!" shouted Rabsy, pointing at the bright colors shimmering above the sea. "And yellow sun and blue sky and everything!"

Far below them, tiny fish swam through secret caves and played hide-and-seek in forests of blue and green seaweed. As the dolphin turned back toward the shore, a group of swifts flew alongside them, skimming the bright water before soaring up into the summer sky. Daisy thought of Flapperton sitting on the windowsill and dreaming of rainbows.

"That was wonderful," she said as the dolphin stopped in the shallow water. She

stroked the dolphin's smooth back and stared out toward the horizon. "The ocean is very big," she whispered. "Will you be all right out there on your own?"

"I won't be on my own," said the dolphin. "Listen."

Daisy leaned sideways until her ear was touching the water, and from somewhere far away, she heard the faintest of clicking sounds.

She smiled. "Are those your friends?"

The dolphin nodded. "They're singing because you found me," he said. "And now they are calling me home."

As Daisy and the rabbits waved good-bye to the dolphin, Daisy noticed something fall off its tail into the water. Bending down, she scooped it up, and there, sitting in the palm of her hand, was someone very familiar.

"Pinchy!" she cried. "What are you doing?"

Pinchy looked up at her and clacked his claws together. "My grandfather crab, he told me that riding on a dolphin feels like magic. So I hitched myself a ride."

"And what did you think?"

Pinchy raised a claw and clacked it like a castanet. "It's magic, all right," he said.

He held out his other claw, and Daisy saw that he was holding a small piece of glass that had been washed smooth by the ocean.

"A gift," he said, "for you."

Then with a cry of "Keep dancing, Daisy!" he scuttled to the edge of her hand, jumped into the water, and disappeared beneath the waves.

"I wonder what

it's for?" said Daisy, turning the glass over in her hand.

"Maybe it's so you don't forget us when you go home," said Raberta.

Daisy stroked her silky ears. "I'll never do that," she said. Then, noticing that both rabbits were still shivering, she gathered them up in her arms and took them to a sunny spot next to the cliff path.

"The walk home should warm you up," she told them. "But if you're still cold, just remember what Pinchy said: 'Keep dancing!'"

Rabsy and Raberta giggled and hugged Daisy's legs. Then they set off, dancing and waving until finally they were lost from sight.

"I always knew you were a good swimmer," said Dad, wrapping Daisy in a towel, "but I didn't know you were *that* good."

"What do you mean?" asked Daisy.

"You looked as though you were riding on a speedboat." Dad chuckled. "The funny thing was it looked like you had a couple of fluffy toys out there with you."

Mom packed away the picnic basket and shook her head. "I think your dad's been sitting in the sun too long," she said.

"I think he has," said Daisy. "I mean, it's obvious that Rabsy and Raberta are rabbits."

"Eh?" said Dad.

Daisy rolled up her towel and smiled.

"Never mind," she said.

As they walked back up the beach, she felt the smooth glass in her pocket.

"Can we go to the shop?" she asked. "I need to get some presents for my friends."

"That's very thoughtful of you," said

Mom. "What did you have in mind?"

"Carrot juice," said Daisy, "and maybe some hazelnut ice cream?"

"Those are some interesting choices," said Dad.

Daisy smiled.

"I've got some interesting friends," she said.

Chapter 7
Raindrops and Rainbows

It had been a wonderful vacation, but it was good to be home again. Daisy hoped her other friends would be as pleased with their presents as Rabsy and Raberta had been with theirs.

"It tastes like raindrops," Raberta had said as she licked carrot juice from her whiskers. "Raindrops made from carrots!"

"*Mmmm,*" said Rabsy, closing his eyes. "Now that's *carroty*!"

As Daisy walked down the lane listening to the bees buzz among the flowers, she heard Boom discussing the weather with Meadowsweet.

"The thing about sunshine," he was saying, "is that it's mainly warm and dry. Whereas rain, on the whole, is a good deal wetter."

"Can't argue with that," said Meadowsweet, looking up at the blue sky. "Although I like the taste of grass after rain. It makes my breath feel fresh and cool."

As Daisy leaned on the gate, Meadowsweet turned and stamped her foot with delight. "Look who's home again!" she whinnied.

"Hello, Meadowsweet," replied Daisy happily. "How would you like something to make your breath feel fresh and cool right now?"

"I wouldn't say no," replied Meadowsweet, trotting over to the gate. "What do
you have? Rain in a bag?"

"Not exactly," said Daisy. "But I think you
might like it, anyway."

She pulled a peppermint from her pocket
and offered it to Meadowsweet. Boom
watched with interest as Meadowsweet
gently snuffled it out of Daisy's hand.

"How does it taste?" he asked.

"Hang on," said Meadowsweet. She
chomped on the mint and shivered.
"It's like a cold drink from a snowy
stream, but without the wet parts.
It's delicious, Daisy!"

"Glad you like it," said Daisy, turning to
Boom. "I've got something for you, too."

She pulled out a small gray pebble and
offered it to him through the gate.

Boom stared at it, sniffed it, and then
looked back at Daisy. "Not to be rude or
anything, but what do I do with it?"

"You eat it," said Daisy.

"Oh," said Boom, sounding disappointed.
"The thing is, I don't really like eating
pebbles. I tried one once, and my teeth
nearly fell out."

Daisy laughed. "It's not a real one, silly,"
she said. "It's a peanut-butter pebble. I
bought a bag of them from the gift shop
near the beach."

Boom sniffed at the pebble again
and licked his lips. "It *does*
smell good," he said.

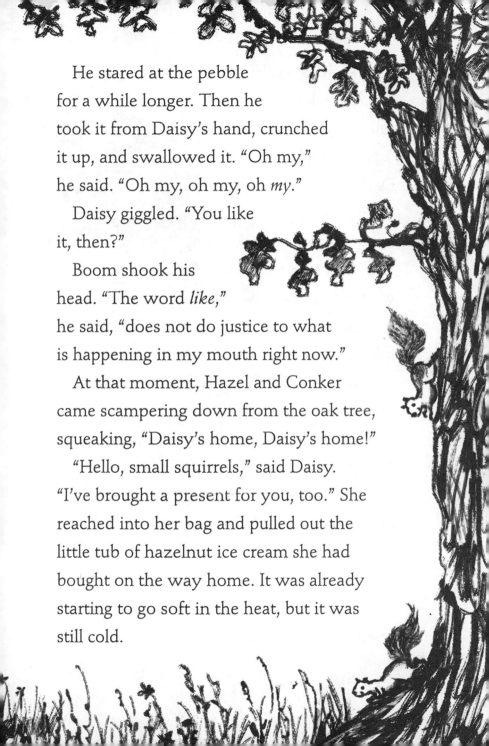

He stared at the pebble
for a while longer. Then he
took it from Daisy's hand, crunched
it up, and swallowed it. "Oh my,"
he said. "Oh my, oh my, oh *my*."

Daisy giggled. "You like
it, then?"

Boom shook his
head. "The word *like*,"
he said, "does not do justice to what
is happening in my mouth right now."

At that moment, Hazel and Conker
came scampering down from the oak tree,
squeaking, "Daisy's home, Daisy's home!"

"Hello, small squirrels," said Daisy.
"I've brought a present for you, too." She
reached into her bag and pulled out the
little tub of hazelnut ice cream she had
bought on the way home. It was already
starting to go soft in the heat, but it was
still cold.

"It's a hat!" exclaimed Hazel as Daisy peeled back the lid. "A hat full of squishy stuff."

"It's not a hat," said Daisy. "It's ice cream."

Conker dipped his nose in and squealed. "It's like those things that fall down in winter!" he cried.

"You mean ducks?" asked Hazel. "Ducks falling over on the ice?"

"No, not ducks. The stuff that comes out of the sky."

"Ducks come out of the sky," said Hazel. "They come out of the sky like anything."

"Snow," said Conker, licking the end of his nose. "It's like snow, but with nuts in it!"

"Nutty snow!" cried Hazel excitedly. She scooped out some ice cream, popped it in her mouth, then jumped in the air and ran around the water trough.

"She always does that when she's excited," explained Conker. "First time she tried a cashew, she went around it twenty-six times."

After a few more circuits, Hazel skipped back across the field, put her paws above her head, and fell back into the long grass.

"I lubbety-*lub* ice cream," she said, staring up at the sky.

"I thought you might," said Daisy, delighted that her presents had been such a success. But then she remembered something.

"Excuse me," she said, "but there's someone else I need to see."

Back in her bedroom, Daisy flung open the window and watched the swifts twisting and turning in the cloudless sky. Bees

buzzed and bumbled in the
flower beds, humming
sweet songs about
honey. As the sun
warmed her face,
she closed her eyes
and felt a soft breeze in
her hair. Then she heard
the flutter of wings and opened her eyes to
see Flapperton the sparrow perched on the
windowsill.

"Hello, Daisy," he
said. "You look happy.
Did you have lots of
adventures?"

"As a matter of fact,
I did," said Daisy. Flapperton's eyes grew
wider and wider as she told him about all
the things she had done.

"But did you fly through any rainbows?"
he asked when she had finished.

"Sort of," said Daisy, remembering the tiny rainbows she had seen on her dolphin ride.

"You are so lucky," said Flapperton. "I would love to do that. It would be like a dream come true. But," he added sadly, "I don't think it will ever happen."

"Well, you never know," said Daisy. "Life is full of surprises. Like the other day, for instance, someone gave me a present, and I didn't know what it was for. But then this morning when I opened the curtains, I found out."

She took the piece of glass that Pinchy had given to her and held it up to the light. And as a shimmering patch of colors appeared on the windowsill, she smiled and said,

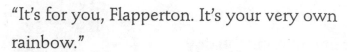

"It's for you, Flapperton. It's your very own rainbow."

And as Flapperton began to flutter back and forth through the bright colors that hovered in the warm summer air, Daisy thought about the rabbits and the dancing crabs and the dolphin swimming out toward the open sea.

She realized then that there was far more magic in the world than most people ever dreamed of.

You just had to know where to look.

For Gill Evans
S. V.

For Elodie
J. M.

Text copyright © 2010 by Steve Voake
Illustrations copyright © 2010 by Jessica Meserve

First U.S. edition 2011

Library of Congress Cataloging-in-Publication Data

Voake, Steve.
Daisy Dawson at the beach / Steve Voake. —1st U.S. ed.
p.   cm.
Summary: Spending the whole summer at the beach, Daisy, who can communicate with animals, and her new friends—a dancing crab and two baby rabbits—join forces to help a dolphin in distress.
ISBN 978-0-7636-5306-4
[1. Human-animal communication—Fiction. 2. Animals—Fiction. 3. Beaches—Fiction. 4. Vacations—Fiction.]   I. Title.
PZ7.V8556Dah 2010
[Fic]—dc22   2010040341

11 12 13 14 15 16 LBM 10 9 8 7 6 5 4 3 2 1

Printed in Melrose Park, IL, U.S.A.

This book was typeset in StempelSchneidler.
The illustrations were done in ink and pencil.

Candlewick Press
99 Dover Street
Somerville, Massachusetts 02144

visit us at www.candlewick.com